# It's Only Murder

### An Adult Comedy Mystery

### With a Number of Immature Moments

## Sam Bobrick

A SAMUEL FRENCH ACTING EDITION

FOUNDED 1830

SAMUELFRENCH.COM
SAMUELFRENCH-LONDON.CO.UK

---

### FOR PRODUCTION ENQUIRIES

#### UNITED STATES AND CANADA
Info@SamuelFrench.com
1-866-598-8449

#### UNITED KINGDOM AND EUROPE
Plays@SamuelFrench-London.co.uk
020-7255-4302

Each title is subject to availability from Samuel French, depending upon country of performance. Please be aware that *IT'S ONLY MURDER* may not be licensed by Samuel French in your territory. Professional and amateur producers should contact the nearest Samuel French office or licensing partner to verify availability.

---

## MUSIC USE NOTE

Licensees are solely responsible for obtaining formal written permission from copyright owners to use copyrighted music in the performance of this play and are strongly cautioned to do so. If no such permission is obtained by the licensee, then the licensee must use only original music that the licensee owns and controls. Licensees are solely responsible and liable for all music clearances and shall indemnify the copyright owners of the play(s) and their licensing agent, Samuel French, against any costs, expenses, losses and liabilities arising from the use of music by licensees. Please contact the appropriate music licensing authority in your territory for the rights to any incidental music.

## IMPORTANT BILLING AND CREDIT REQUIREMENTS

If you have obtained performance rights to this title, please refer to your licensing agreement for important billing and credit requirements.

*IT'S ONLY MURDER* was first presented as a staged reading as part of the Seasoned Readings series at the Writers Guild of America, West in Los Angeles, CA on March 31, 2014. The performance was directed by Susan Morgenstern. The cast was as follows:

**JEROME TEPPEL** .............................. Richard Horvitz

**FRANCINE TEPPEL**.............................. Devon Sorvari

**LENORE FRANKLIN**............................. Bridget Flanery

**SID DECKER** ..................................... Philip Proctor

## THE CAST

## TIME

The Present.

## PRODUCTION NOTE

The play has no formal set and is done with appropriate lighting and a minimum of furniture.

# ACT I

## Scene One

*(TIME: The present. Evening.)*

*(PLACE: The **TEPPEL** living room.)*

*(AT RISE: **JEROME TEPPEL**, a somewhat uptight CPA in his late thirties is sitting at a desk and going through his monthly credit card statement, checking the charges against a stack of receipts he has in front of him. After routinely going through several of them and marking them off the statement, he sees something on the statement that confuses him.)*

**JEROME.** What the hell is this?

*(He then searches through the receipts until he finds the one he's looking for.)*

Oh, my God.

*(Calling)*

Francine! Francine!

*(Looks at the receipt again)*

Jesus Christ! This is crazy.

*(Calling again)*

Francine!

*(Louder and more impatient. He turns and calls upstage:)*

Francine!

(**FRANCINE TEPPEL,** *an attractive, seemingly sweet, innocently naive and concerned woman in her late twenties enters the room. She is in a bathrobe.*)

FRANCINE. I'm sorry, Jerome, I was getting ready for bed. Something wrong?

JEROME. Yes. Very wrong.

I was going through this months's credit card bill and there was a charge from a place called Larry's Gun Shop.

FRANCINE. Yes. And?

JEROME. I knew it had to be some kind of mistake. So I went through this month's receipts and here it is. Larry's Gun Shop. Three hundred and seventy-two dollars and eighty-four cents for a thirty-eight Smith and Wesson revolver.

*(Holds out the receipt to her)*

See, here's the receipt.

FRANCINE. Yes. And?

JEROME. What do you mean "yes and"?

FRANCINE. I know how important it is for you to have receipts for everything so I always make sure I get one.

JEROME. Damn it, Francine, you seem to be missing the point. You bought a gun.

FRANCINE. I did. Yes, I know.

JEROME. Why?

FRANCINE. Two reasons. First of all, I know how you love for me to buy things on sale and it was marked down from four-fifty. Of course the bullets were extra but I even got twenty percent off on those. Wasn't that wonderful Jerome?

JEROME. Not necessarily. And your second reason?

FRANCINE. Well, Frankly, I thought we need to have one in the house.

JEROME. Why? I hate guns. Just seeing one makes me nauseous.

**FRANCINE.** I know. But these are not good times Jerome. There are more home robberies than ever before, more stick ups at ATM's, more drive by shootings. Our streets are swarming with pedophiles and rapists and with police protection stretched to the limit, it's a very dangerous world and I think one that's getting worse every day.

**JEROME.** I see. So basically what you're saying is that I'm not adequately terrified.

**FRANCINE.** You're an accountant, Jerome. You live in a whole other world. I thought it was about time one of us approached this troubling situation in a realistic way.

**JEROME.** First of all, and I'm sorry I have to keep reminding you of this, Francine, I'm not just an accountant, I'm a CPA. There's a difference. Like the difference between a doctor and a dentist. A mother is always prouder of the doctor.

**FRANCINE.** And you're the...

**JEROME.** The doctor! Yes. Secondly, what the hell do you know about shooting a gun?

**FRANCINE.** There's really not that much to know. Larry, the gun shop owner, showed me how in just a few minutes. You flip the chamber open, put in the bullets, flip the chamber back, bang bang someone's dead. No big deal. A five year old kid can learn how to do it.

**JEROME.** Yes, and unfortunately they do. Still, I'm really surprised by this. You never mentioned you wanted to buy a gun before. And we always discuss major purchases together.

**FRANCINE.** Of course, Jerome, but I was under the impression that a major purchase is something like a car or a refrigerator. This was just a tiny little gun and frankly I felt very good leaving the store with it.

**JEROME.** They gave you the gun the same day? No background check?

**FRANCINE.** No, Larry said that if a customer has an honest face that was good enough for him, which was frightening in itself because I realized if I could get one that easily, any nut could get one. Scary, isn't it?

**JEROME.** More than you know. Okay, so where is this gun?

**FRANCINE.** Here's another sticky part of that story. I lost it.

**JEROME.** You lost the gun?

**FRANCINE.** Yes. The very same day I bought it. That's why I didn't bother bringing it up. You see, after I bought the gun, I had a ton of other errands to do, the mall, the dry cleaners, the grocery store, and so on and so on and when I came home and unloaded the car, it was gone.

Obviously, rushing around to do all the things I had to do, I must have accidentally left the car unlocked and someone stole it.

**JEROME.** That's terrible.

**FRANCINE.** I know. That's why you really need a gun. To prevent these kind of crimes.

**JEROME.** Well, I hope you reported it to the police. I think that's the first thing you're supposed to do when you discover a firearm is missing.

**FRANCINE.** Well, I haven't done that yet but here's what I was planning. I'm going back to Larry's Gun Shop, explain to him what happened and see if he'll give me another one at the same low, low price and maybe he could also handle all the paper work that goes with reporting my lost gun.

**JEROME.** Whoa, whoa, whoa! You're not buying another gun.

**FRANCINE.** No? I need to be honest, Jerome, since I lost the one I bought, I'm feeling very vulnerable.

**JEROME.** Francine, we've been married ten months now and while at times I have found you a bit flaky, buying a gun has taken things a bit past flaky.

**FRANCINE.** You think so?

**JEROME**. Yes, I do.

**FRANCINE**. You're annoyed with me, aren't you?

**JEROME**. Yes, I am.

*(She sits down and starts to sniffle.)*

**FRANCINE**. I can't do anything right.

**JEROME**. No, no. That's not true. Sometimes you can.

**FRANCINE**. Our marriage isn't working, is it Jerome?

**JEROME**. Of course it is.

**FRANCINE**. No, no I sense it. You think I'm a scatterbrain, don't you? Admit it.

**JEROME**. No, not a scatterbrain. Sometimes…sensibly challenged. How's that? Better?

**FRANCINE**. No. No, it isn't better. I want to be a good wife to you, Jerome, but for my own self worth I need to be my own person in this marriage. I refuse to go on with my every move being questioned, my every decision coming under your scrutiny. I need to be an equal partner in this relationship. Otherwise, Jerome, we are doomed as a couple and as you recall, I refused to sign a pre-nup.

**JEROME**. *(Thinking about that for a moment)* That's true, isn't it. Smart move on your part. Okay. I'm sorry, Francine. Maybe you're right. I am a bit controlling and maybe I do need to loosen the reins. So, okay, how's this?

*(Puts his arm around her to comfort her)*

As of right now this marriage is going to be one hundred percent fair.

As of right this minute I, Jerome Teppel, CPA, promise that I will no longer be constantly looking over my wife's shoulder, always criticizing her wifely efforts to make our life together the wonderful relationship I had hoped it would be, even though some of the things she's done in the past have been questionable, if not plain out and out stupid. There! Satisfied?

FRANCINE. Yes. Much more. Thank you, Jerome. You'll see. I'm going to be a very responsible, practical and thoughtful partner.

JEROME. I'm sure of it. Now is there anything else I should know?

FRANCINE. As a matter of fact, while we're on the subject of family expenditures, next month there'll be a six hundred and fifty dollar charge from the Crystal Springs Cemetery.

JEROME. This is going to be a doozie, isn't it Francine?

FRANCINE. Well, you know, Jerome, how the cost of everything keeps rising? I received a solicitation call from one of the sales people at the cemetery who told me that for only a six hundred and fifty dollar deposit, we could reserve a burial plot for the next twenty years at this years low, low price. Knowing how important it is to you that I constantly look for money saving opportunities, I reserved one.

JEROME. One? You reserved one? Only one?

FRANCINE. It made the most sense.
You see with your being nine years older than I am and with men known to die at least ten years before their wives, chances are excellent you're going to go way, way before me and by then who knows if I'm going to want to live in this area anymore.

JEROME. (Nods. A beat.) Uh huh. Let me recap this, Francine. You bought a gun to protect us and a cemetery plot for me to save money for us, yes, I guess it all makes sense.

FRANCINE. Of course it does. Plus I no longer am faced with having to make last minute funeral arrangements for you during my time of bereavement which, for the past few months, has been a constant burden on my mind just thinking about it.

(Kisses him on the cheek)

Well, I'm off to bed.

**JEROME.** I'm happy to hear that.

**FRANCINE.** *(Starts off then stops and turns)* Oh, one more thing, Jerome. Are you going to be around Thursday evening?

**JEROME.** Yes, why, I'm afraid to ask.

**FRANCINE.** Well, a lawyer from the firm that handles your estate will be coming over with a few documents you need to sign.

**JEROME.** Documents? What kind of documents I'm even more afraid to ask?

**FRANCINE.** Well, since you're a married man now with new responsibilities, meaning me, and since we are now finally taking a long, hard look at the future, I've arranged for your Will to be amended so that when you do bite the big one or are incapacitated in any way, the financial control of your estate will be smoothly and without question, transferred to your heirs, meaning me, so that she, I being she, will not have to go through any unnecessary legal hassles or costs and will continue to be properly provided for in a way that a loving CPA as yourself would want her to be. Well, don't stay up too late Jerome. I'm quite relieved we had this little discussion. Good night.

*(She kisses **JEROME** on the cheek and exits. **JEROME** faces the audience. He is stunned. He starts to count on his fingers.)*

**JEROME.** A gun, a cemetery plot, changes to my Will… Holy shit, what did I get myself into?

*(Blackout)*

## Scene Two

*(TIME: Several days later. Lunchtime.)*

*(PLACE: A park bench.)*

**(LENORE FRANKLIN,** *an attractive woman in her early-thirties sits on the bench, obviously waiting for someone.* **LENORE** *is a very outspoken, straight-to-the-point kind of woman. Right now she seems concerned, troubled. She sees someone and waves.)*

**LENORE.** Jerome! Over here!

**(JEROME** *approaches her. He is carrying a bag with their lunch.)*

**JEROME.** I'm sorry, I'm late, Lenore. There was a line at the deli and it seemed to take forever.

*(He starts unpacking the bag which consists of two sandwiches and two cups of coffee.)*

**LENORE.** I'm so glad you were able to make it, Jerome. I know it's strange, my wanting to meet here since we live right next door to each other and are fairly good friends, but I can't take any chances. I need to be very discreet about this which, I think I am being.

**JEROME.** Yes. Well, whatever the problem is, it seemed to be very urgent.

**LENORE.** Urgent and uncomfortable. Very uncomfortable.

**(JEROME** *hands her a sandwich.)*

**JEROME.** Here you are. A turkey sandwich for you and a roast beef for me.

**LENORE.** Thank you. It's very sweet of you to bring lunch for us.

**JEROME.** No problem at all. Besides, I have to grab a bite whenever I can. It's tax season and as usual I'm overwhelmed with more new government forms to fill out, more new government regulations to read, more new irresponsible clients not giving me the right information…it's murder.

**LENORE.** I know the feeling. The insurance business is no piece of cake either. People late with their premium payment, people making fraudulent claims, people constantly threatening to sue us because they failed to read the small print and didn't realize how few things their policies cover...the day to day stress is overwhelming.

**JEROME.** I thought you were just a receptionist.

**LENORE.** I am but I have to open all the mail in the morning and this is what I'm faced with. Believe me, if there was anyway I could dump that job I'd do it in a minute but when you're married to a dead beat, as my husband Anthony has proven himself to be, I have to think twice about that. If I didn't walk away with a nice settlement from my first marriage I don't know how we would be able to afford our lifestyle which is the only reason I think that jerk married me in the first place.

*(Bites into sandwich)*

Oh, my god, there's mayonnaise on this sandwich. I hate mayonnaise.

**JEROME.** Really? I'm almost positive you said turkey with mayo.

**LENORE.** *(Annoyed)* No, I didn't say turkey with mayo. I would never say anything with mayo. Especially turkey.

And I know I said no mayo because I'll always say no mayo even when ordering something they never put mayo on.

**JEROME.** I'm so sorry. Well, why don't we switch sandwiches? Do you mind mustard? I have roast beef with just mustard on it.

**LENORE.** Yes, I think that will be much better. I actually like mustard a lot. That's what you should have put on the turkey. Here, I'll take yours and you take mine. That works out much better. Thank you very much.

*(They switch sandwiches. **JEROME**, with disgust, looks at the one he was just handed which now has a big bite out of it.)*

**JEROME**. Sure. Anyway, you said it was very important that we meet in private.

**LENORE**. Very. I didn't want Anthony to find out I was talking to you. He's quite paranoid you know.

**JEROME**. No, I didn't know.

**LENORE**. Yes. Even more so than I am.

**JEROME**. So then this is a problem concerning you and Anthony?

**LENORE**. Partly. It also concerns you too, Jerome. Actually, very much you.

*(Bites into **JEROME**'s sandwich)*

Ech! Yuck! I can't eat this. This is practically raw.

**JEROME**. Yes, well, it's rare. That's the way roast beef usually comes at a deli. Very rare.

**LENORE**. This is more than very rare, Jerome. You have to be a cannibal to eat this. Let me try my turkey sandwich again.

*(Takes the sandwich out of **JEROME**'s hands)*

Turkey!

*(Takes a bite, chews it then holds up the roast beef)*

Roast beef!

*(Takes a bite, chews it then hands it to **JEROME**)*

I think I'll stick with the turkey. But next time, please, no mayo on anything, ever.

**JEROME**. I'll keep that in mind.

**LENORE**. Except for chicken salad or egg salad because then the mayo is in it, not on it. I actually *like* mayo when it's in it and not on it.

**JEROME**. Really?

**LENORE**. Yes. It's not a bad idea for you to remember that. Now, where were we?

**JEROME.** I have no idea.

**LENORE.** Oh, yes. About my husband and your wife.

**JEROME.** Francine?

**LENORE.** Yes. And my husband, Anthony. They're having an affair.

**JEROME.** You're kidding me?

**LENORE.** I'm afraid not.

> *(Sips on her coffee)*

Oh, damn it. You put cream and sugar in here.

**JEROME.** Well, I thought you said a coffee reg.

**LENORE.** A reg, yes. But I meant a reg like in regular size. Coffee comes black, you know. That's the way I like it. If I wanted cream and sugar I would have said cream and sugar. I can't drink this, it's awful.

**JEROME.** I'm sorry. Actually, mine is black. Why don't we just switch.

**LENORE.** You don't mind?

**JEROME.** No, not at all. I would just like to get back to this conversation. You just hit me with some very upsetting news, that my wife and your husband are having an affair.

**LENORE.** Yes. I'm almost sure of it.

**JEROME.** What do you mean *almost* sure?

**LENORE.** We live next door to each other, Jerome. My husband being an artist, a very romantic profession, your wife being an unhappy housewife, both of them home alone, what more do you need to know?

**JEROME.** Wait a minute. Hold on. What do you mean my wife is unhappy?

**LENORE.** Because if she was happy she wouldn't be having an affair. Look, you choose to be blind to what's going on, but I don't.

> *(Sips the coffee)*

Oh, my God. This coffee is too hot. It'll never cool off in time to drink it. Let me try the other one again with the cream and sugar.

**JEROME.** Goddamn it, Lenore. Before you put one more friggen thing in your mouth, for God's sake finish telling me what you came here to tell me.

**LENORE.** Jerome, Jerome, Jerome. How dimwitted are you? We're neighbors. And although I've always felt you were a very difficult man, as well as being somewhat arrogant, judgmental and for reasons that totally escape me, extremely anti-social, still, you must admit we do have contact with each other. Sometimes we go out to dinner, sometimes a barbecue in our back yards…

**JEROME.** Jesus Christ, Lenore, I know what we do together! Can you please, please get to this affair stuff before I lose my mind!

**LENORE.** Jerome, Jerome, Jerome. Don't you see the way they look at each other, the way their eyes brighten when they meet, the way their faces light up? Haven't you noticed any of that?

**JEROME.** No, not at all.

(**LENORE** *places her cup next to* **JEROME** *and takes his from his hand.*)

**LENORE.** Well, I have and I've been noticing it more and more. I can only imagine what happens when we're at work and they're home alone.

**JEROME.** Imagine? That's the key word. Imagine. This accusation could all be just that, a case of "imagine".

**LENORE.** Well, then, how's this. The other day I went into Anthony's studio. He is now in the midst of painting a nude portrait of your wife.

**JEROME.** No?

**LENORE.** Yes. Full frontal. You see everything. Her no-no's and her yahoo.

**JEROME.** *(Shocked)* Her yahoo?

**LENORE.** Her muffin, her love basket, her clam can. Whatever you guys call it.

JEROME. *(Now very upset)* I know what we call it! A nude painting! Oh, my God. She never mentioned she was doing anything like that? Are you sure it's her? Maybe he's doing it from a photograph. Her face and someone else's body. That's done all the time. I'm willing to bet it's not Francine's body.

LENORE. There's a birth mark on her left breast in the shape of a one legged duck.

JEROME. That's Francine's body.

LENORE. You bet it is. I also found something else in his studio that has me very, very worried.

JEROME. Like what?

(**FRANCINE** *puts down her coffee cup, opens her purse and pulls out a gun.*)

LENORE. Like this. A brand new thirty-eight Smith and Wesson revolver. Anthony has never owned a gun in his life.

JEROME. I think I'm going to throw up.

LENORE. Good. That's the reaction I was hoping for. By the way, did you happen to bring a dessert? I always like to finish my meal with something sweet. I like almost anything but a prune danish, but if that's all you brought, I'll try my best.

(*The lights dim.* **LENORE** *continues eating.* **JEROME** *has a confused, worried look on his face.*)

You'd better drink your coffee before it gets cold.

(*Blackout*)

## Scene Three

*(TIME: That night.)*

*(PLACE: The* **TEPPEL** *living room. Another area.)*

**(JEROME** *and* **FRANCINE** *are sitting in two arm chairs angled so that they almost face each other as well as the audience.* **FRANCINE** *is reading a magazine and humming softly to herself.* **JEROME** *stares at her for several beats.)*

**JEROME.** *(Finally)* I had lunch with Lenore today.

**FRANCINE.** *(Not really interested)* Oh. Lenore from next door.

**JEROME.** Yes, Lenore from next door. She insisted on talking to me about something very, very upsetting.

**FRANCINE.** Oh. That's too bad.

**JEROME.** Do you want to know what it was about?

**FRANCINE.** Well, I'd say it was about their marriage, if anything.

**JEROME.** Yes, as a matter of fact, it was about their marriage.

**FRANCINE.** Well, it's not going to work out. That marriage is too far gone to be saved.

**JEROME.** Oh. You know that for a fact?

**FRANCINE.** She's horrible to him. Anthony has been complaining to me about it for months.

**JEROME.** Complaining to you? Isn't that a bit strange?

**FRANCINE.** No, not at all. We're neighbors. Every now and then we have coffee together and we talk about our problems, you know the way a lot of women do, except in Anthony's case he's a man.

**JEROME.** Yes, he is a man, isn't he. And just what problems do you two talk about?

**FRANCINE.** Well, let's start with Anthony's. Number one, he finds Lenore very difficult to live with. She's never happy with anything. They go to a restaurant she complains about the food, they go to a movie, she complains about the seat, they go to a marriage counselor, she complains about their marriage.

**JEROME.** But that's what you go to a marriage counselor for?

**FRANCINE.** Yes, but he hears it at home all the time, why does he have to hear it there? Number two. His career. Just because he's been painting for twenty years and hasn't sold anything yet is no need to keep calling him a loser. Look at Van Gogh. He never made a living until after he was dead.

**JEROME.** I know. Tax wise it made good sense.

**FRANCINE.** Number three. She's extremely suspicious of him. She has to know where he is, what he's doing every minute of the day. He finds it suffocating. Quite honestly, so would I.

**JEROME.** I'll bet you would.

**FRANCINE.** And number four, and I think this is the deal breaker. He no longer enjoys having sex with her and more than anything else in life, Anthony loves sex.

**JEROME.** He does?

**FRANCINE.** Oh, my God, does he ever. Any time, any where, any place, he's ready. On the kitchen table, in a hall closet, on the bathroom floor, outside in the bushes. His favorite is the back seat of his car, yet with her he feels nothing.

**JEROME.** She's lucky. Fornicating with that guy, she could end up in a wheel chair. So with all this pent up passion, who does he have sex with?

**FRANCINE.** Rumor has it, it's someone in the neighborhood.

**JEROME.** Right now that would be my guess too. And what were your complaints to him about your life with me?

**FRANCINE.** Oh, just little things. Your extreme thriftiness, your lack of trust, the regret I hear in your voice when we have in-depth discussions like this.

**JEROME.** Uh huh. And what about *our* sex life? Any complaints about that?

**FRANCINE.** No. Not really. I mean for what it is, I guess our sex life is okay.

**JEROME.** Just okay?

**FRANCINE.** Please, Jerome. For a CPA that's a very high mark.

**JEROME.** And so you and Anthony discuss all these things.

**FRANCINE.** Well, yes. You and Lenore are gone all day and we need to talk to someone or we'll both go crazy. Like I said, it's basically a good neighbor relationship.

**JEROME.** And that's all?

**FRANCINE.** Yes, of course that's all. Please don't tell me you're having a problem with that?

**JEROME.** I am. A big problem. I'm not sure a good neighbor relationship includes posing in the nude for your good neighbor.

**FRANCINE.** Oh, my. You know about the painting?

**JEROME.** Yes. Thanks to *my* good neighbor Lenore, I know about the painting.

**FRANCINE.** Oh, damn her! I wanted it to be a surprise.

**JEROME.** Well, good news, it was. A very big surprise.

**FRANCINE.** Honey, do you know what next month is? It's your fortieth birthday. That was going to be my gift to you. Since you're aware of every penny I spend, I didn't want you to know what I was buying you so I came up with this idea of a nude portrait and since Anthony and I have this very good neighbor relationship, he offered to do it for free.

**JEROME.** And so you posed naked for him?

**FRANCINE.** Oh, come on Jerome. He's an artist. He's seen hundreds of nude models. It's like going to a gynecologist. He knows what all the parts of a woman's body look like so what's the big deal? I thought a nude picture of me would be a great birthday present to give you. I was hoping you would hang it up in your office and maybe it would encourage you to start coming home earlier than you do. But if you think there is something suspicious going on between me and Anthony, you're one hundred percent wrong because there is nothing, absolutely nothing lewd or indecent or the least bit improper about our friendship. Now, before I let myself become too annoyed with this conversation, is there anything more you feel a need to bring up?

**JEROME.** Yes. One more thing. This!

*(He produces the gun.)*

What the hell was he doing with this?

**FRANCINE.** Oh, my. That looks just like the gun I bought. Where did you find it?

**JEROME.** I didn't. Lenore did. In Anthony's studio. I do believe you two have a lot of explaining to do. A lot of explaining.

*(**FRANCINE** is speechless. The lights dim.)*

*(Blackout)*

## Scene Four

*(TIME: Several days later. Lunchtime.)*

*(PLACE:* **SID DECKER***'s second floor shabby office.)*

*(***SID DECKER***, a seedy Private Detective in his forties, who has obviously seen better days, is behind a desk. He wears a suit that has also seen better days. His shirt collar is open, his tie loosened and he could use a shave. Behind him is a large framed window that overlooks a rundown neighborhood. There are two chairs near the desk.* **LENORE** *sits in one of them. She is pouring her heart out to* **SID***.)*

**LENORE.** I never thought that bastard would cheat on me. You can't imagine how good I've been to him, how patient and understanding I am. That no good, ungrateful, rotten, son of a bitch.

*(About to cry)*

Oh, God, you have no idea how much I love him.

**SID.** Are you about to cry, Mrs Franklin?

**LENORE.** *(Fighting tears)* I believe I am.

**SID.** Well don't. It's enough I have to listen to crap like this all day long, but I really can't handle the bullshit tears that go with it.

**LENORE.** I'm sorry. I'm a very emotional person, Mr. Decker.

**SID.** Yeah, you and Jack the Ripper. Cut the shit, Mrs. Franklin. You don't need to play any games with me. I'm up to my ass in cheaters. Cheating husbands, cheating wives, cheating cheaters. You want to hire me to investigate your suspicions about your husband and neighbor, that I do and do well.

But don't expect me to get caught up emotionally in your stupid, moronic, petty life because the bottom line is that I don't care a skunk's crap about any of you.

**LENORE.** You're a cold fish aren't you, Mr. Decker? Colorful but cold.

**SID.** Yes, and I'm also happy to add, a huge asshole. This is a rotten, stinking business and I'm in it strictly for the rotten, stinking money. Everything else means the big zero to me.

**LENORE.** I see. Well, let me be blatantly honest with you as you have been with me, Mr. Decker. You are a rude and gross man and I find your horrendous lack of compassion as refreshing as a gas station bathroom that reeks of thirty-day-old urine. That being said, it's more than obvious I've come to the right man. By the way, I'm going to call you Sid if you don't mind. Calling you Mr. Decker seems much too respectful and gives one the false assumption that maybe there's a touch of human decency in that body.

*(JEROME enters with a bag containing lunch.)*

**JEROME.** Hi, I got here as fast as I could.

**LENORE.** It's about time. Sid, this is Jerome Teppel, the husband of that bitch I thought was my best friend. Jerome, this is Sid Decker, the private detective it looks like we're going to hire. He has a quality that I find extremely delightful – a total lack of charm.

*(JEROME extends his hand.)*

**JEROME.** Nice to meet you.

**SID.** I'm sorry. I make it a point not to shake a person's hand unless they're holding a check for me in the other one.

**JEROME.** *(Withdrawing his hand)* Totally understandable.

*(Unpacks the lunch)*

I hope you don't mind our eating in your office.

**SID.** No. Go right ahead. In fact, I'll join you.

*(He pulls out a bottle of whiskey and a glass from his desk drawer and pours himself a tall drink)*

**LENORE.** Oh, god, Sid. You're so "film noir" it's sickening.

(JEROME *watches as* SID *puts the glass to his lips.*)

SID. In case you're wondering if I'm an alcoholic, I am. It's the only way I can stomach you people.

*(He takes a large gulp.)*

JEROME. That's very comforting to know.

LENORE. *(Impatient)* The sandwiches, Jerome.

JEROME. Right.

*(Hands her a sandwich)*

Here you are, tuna salad for you and chicken salad for me with the mayo mixed *in* and not *on.*

LENORE. Tuna salad? I didn't say tuna salad.

JEROME. I'm sure you said tuna salad.

LENORE. I did not. I said anything but tuna salad. Don't you ever listen?

JEROME. All right. I'm not a fan of tuna salad but I'll give you my chicken salad and I'll take your tuna.

LENORE. I'm not thrilled with chicken salad either but anything's better than tuna.

SID. *(Annoyed)* Can we get on with this?

JEROME. Sure. One more second. Let me get these out.

*(Takes out two cups of coffee from the bag and places them on the desk)*

LENORE. *(Takes the sandwich out of the paper wrapper)* Damn it. It's on pumpernickel. No one eats a chicken salad on pumpernickel.

JEROME. So don't eat it. I really don't give a damn anymore, Lenore.

LENORE. Touchy, touchy.

*(Takes her drink)*

Is this coffee?

JEROME. Yes, black. And I put in ice cubes so it won't be too hot.

**LENORE.** Well, actually with chicken salad, a soda would have been a better choice. You really have no imagination, do you, Jerome?

**JEROME.** Right now I'm imaging you under a bus. How's that?

**LENORE.** A bit hostile, but I guess to the point.

*(Bites into the sandwich then spits it out)*

There's celery in this chicken salad.

**JEROME.** Yes. I know. I asked for it. I like chicken salad with celery.

**LENORE.** I hate celery. I never eat celery. Give me back the tuna.

**JEROME.** Go screw yourself. I'm eating this sandwich and that's that.

**LENORE.** I want my tuna, Jerome.

**JEROME.** No!

**SID.** Okay, okay. Stop. Stop right now! If I hear one more word about those sandwiches you're gonna find them shoved up your rectums.

**LENORE.** Oh, really?

**SID.** Yeah, really.

**LENORE.** Interesting.

**SID.** I need another drink.

*(Pours himself another drink)*

**LENORE.** Look at the man, Jerome. A hard boiled, hard drinking, miserable, classless excuse for a human being.

We could not have found a more perfect private detective no matter how much we lowered our standards.

**SID.** Can we get on with it?

**LENORE.** Right. Now, I told Sid everything, about why I think our spouses are cheating but I think you should tell him about the gun and the rest of the stuff.

**SID.** There's gun stuff? I charge extra for gun stuff.

JEROME. Yes, but it seems like it can all be explained and it isn't as bad as I first thought. See, my wife bought a gun, a thirty-eight Smith and Wesson revolver.

SID. Nice weapon. Perfect for convenience store hold ups.

JEROME. I'm sure she'll be happy to know that. Anyway, not only did she buy a gun, she also bought a cemetery plot for me and insisted I amend my will just in case I might need that cemetery plot a little sooner than expected. Now, although she said she lost the gun and I was still a little nervous about all those other things, I was willing to give her the benefit of the doubt until...

*(Takes a deep breath)*

LENORE. Until I found the gun in my husband's studio. A little more intriguing, huh, Sid? I'll bet you don't get many cases like this every day.

SID. Shut up and let him finish.

JEROME. Anyway, I confronted her husband about the gun the very next night.

SID. And?

JEROME. He said he found the gun on the street, which my wife could have easily dropped when she brought in the groceries. He had no idea whose it was, but as an artist he was fascinated by it and decided to do a painting of it. You know, like Andy Warhol did with a soup can. He decided to do the same thing with a gun.

LENORE. Jesus, Jerome, this sandwich tastes like shit.

SID. Will you shut the fuck up.

LENORE. Sorry for breathing.

SID. By any chance, did you see the painting of the gun?

JEROME. Not only did I see it, I bought it for a hundred and fifty bucks. He said if I wasn't a neighbor he'd have to charge me twice that. Well, my nature is such that I couldn't possibly pass up such a terrific deal.

LENORE. Anthony was very excited. It was the first painting he ever sold. He took me out that night for dinner and we had the best lobster I ever had soaked in garlic butter that was not to be believed.

**SID**. I'm thrilled. So maybe there isn't anything going on between the two of them.

**LENORE**. Not so fast. There was one more thing. Tell him about the other painting, Jerome.

**JEROME**. *(embarrassed)* Well, I... I mean Francine... She... I mean they...

**LENORE**. My husband is doing a painting of his wife in the nude.

**SID**. He's not wearing clothes?

**JEROME**. No, she's not wearing clothes. Actually, he showed me that painting too. It wasn't bad. He still needed to do a little more work on her...her biscuit.

**SID**. Her biscuit?

**LENORE**. Yeah, Sid. Her honey tunnel, her hootchy cootchy, her happy snapper. Don't pretend you never heard those expressions before.

**SID**. I have, but coming from you they've lost their sweetness.

**JEROME**. Anyway, I started to feel really stupid. Maybe they weren't cheating, maybe they weren't plotting... I actually ended up apologizing to both of them. But...

**SID**. But what?

**JEROME**. But later that night, I started to get these doubts again, especially when I woke up at three in the morning and discovered my wife, Francine, wasn't in bed.

**LENORE**. Where was she?

**JEROME**. When I went to look for her, she was just coming in through the back door. She said she was outside for an hour or two just looking at the moon.

**SID**. And you didn't believe her?

**JEROME**. I peeked outside. There was no moon. And then I noticed that she reeked of lobster and garlic.

**SID**. And what was your husband doing at three in the morning, Mrs. Franklin?

**LENORE**. I don't know. I have trouble sleeping so I take sleeping pills. For eight hours a night, I'm out cold.

(**SID** *rises and begins to walk around.*)

**SID**. So it's very possible the two of them could very well have been together engaging in a sordid round of hanky-panky-hide-the-wanky.

**LENORE**. Hanky-panky-hide-the-wanky? Oh, Sid. I never would have guessed you went to high school.

**SID**. Screw off. Okay Jerome, so where's the gun now?

**JEROME**. I have it. It's in my desk drawer. I was hoping to get my money back for it, but Larry's Gun Shop has a no return policy on sale items. By any chance you wouldn't be interested in buying it from me? I'll make you a good deal.

**SID**. You hold on to the gun. Those two are obviously playing a hand. I need to see what other cards they've got up their sleeves.

**LENORE**. "Cards up their sleeves, playing a hand"... Jerome, I could not be more convinced that we hired the right dick.

**SID**. Look, for now, I want you two to go on with your lives like there's nothing wrong. In the meantime, I'll poke around. If there is something going on between them I'll soon have pictures to prove it.

**JEROME**. Pictures?

**SID**. With today's technology and a little ingenuity, I can get pictures of anyone, anywhere. Check out my web site. I got pictures of guys cheating with chicks, guys cheating with guys, chicks cheating with chicks. I got threesomes, foursomes, group, got it all. I get over ten thousand hits a month. God, how people love smut.

**JEROME**. Hold it a minute. You're going to put a picture of my wife making love to...

(*Pointing to* **LENORE**)

...her husband on the internet?

**SID.** Yeah, providing I can capture them in some hot positions. If they're just into missionary you can forget it. I have a very sophisticated audience that demands sophisticated perversion.

**LENORE.** Speaking for my husband I can guarantee you he won't let you down.

**SID.** Good.

**JEROME.** Wait! Not so fast. I need to think about this. It's really not a nice thing to do.

**SID.** Don't be a shmuck, Jerome. The problem isn't that they may be having an affair. The problem is they may be planning to kill you.

**LENORE.** Sid's right. We're not dealing with decent, moral people such as you and I. We're dealing with a couple of crumbs like Sid.

**JEROME.** Okay, okay. I don't like it but I'll go along with it.

(*Indicates* **LENORE**)

Do all the necessary paper work with her. I gotta get out of here before I start feeling more disgusted than I do.

(*He throws his sandwich in the bag and starts to leave.*)

**LENORE.** Wait a minute, Jerome. What about dessert? I hope you brought something this time.

**JEROME.** Oh, yeah. I forgot. Sorry.

(**JEROME** *puts his hand in the bag, searches around for a second and then pulls out a wrapped Danish and hands it to* **LENORE**.)

Here!

**LENORE.** Oh, thanks.

(*She unwraps it.*)

A prune Danish! I told you I hate prune Danish.

**JEROME.** I know. That's why I bought it. Gotta go.

(*He exits.*)

**SID.** I get the feeling he hates your guts.

**LENORE.** On the contrary. He actually likes me more than he knows. He's just doing everything he can to fight the feeling. I have good instincts about things like that.

**SID.** Just the way you have good instincts about me.

**LENORE.** Exactly.

*(Bites into the Danish)*

This prune Danish isn't half bad.

*(Holds out the Danish to* **SID***)*

Want a bite?

*(Blackout)*

## Scene Five

*(TIME: Middle of the night.)*

*(PLACE: The* **TEPPEL** *living room.)*

*(The stage is dark. We hear the doorbell, then frantic pounding on the door, then the doorbell again. Someone is desperate to get in.)*

*(Lights up as* **JEROME** *and* **FRANCINE** *enter the living room in bathrobes and go to the front door.* **JEROME** *opens it. A hysterical* **LENORE** *rushes in. She is also in her bathrobe.)*

**LENORE.** Oh, my, God! Oh, my God!

**JEROME.** What's wrong.

**LENORE.** Oh, Thank you Jesus-God-in-Heaven! I did not take a sleeping pill tonight.

**JEROME.** So?

**LENORE.** So I woke up just a little bit ago. And Anthony wasn't in bed.

**FRANCINE.** He wasn't?

**LENORE.** No, he wasn't.

**JEROME.** So?

**LENORE.** So I went to look for him in his studio. I was sure he was with that bitch wife of yours.

**FRANCINE.** What? What are you talking about?

**LENORE.** Don't deny it. I know you two have been sleeping together.

**FRANCINE.** Oh, come on Anthony and I are just good friends and that's all. I swear, just good friends.

**LENORE.** Oh, really. And whose panties are these?

*(Produces a pair of bikini panties)*

**FRANCINE.** *(Taking panties)* Oh, my. I wondered where they were.

Where did you find them?

**LENORE.** In Anthony's studio. Explain that bitch.

**FRANCINE.** Quite easily. I obviously left them there. He was putting the finishing touches on my portrait.

**JEROME.** I told you that this afternoon, Lenore. He still had work to do on her…whoopee.

**FRANCINE.** My what?

**LENORE.** Oh, grow up. Your fuzz box, your sugar nest, your wang warmer. He was clutching these in his hand when I found him dead on the floor with a bullet hole in his head.

**FRANCINE.** *(Hysterical)* Anthony, dead. No, no, no! Oh, my god! Oh, my god! It can't be!
Tell me it can't be! Please, tell me it can't be!

**JEROME.** *(Accusing)* You *were* having an affair with him!

**FRANCINE.** *(Pulling herself together rather quickly)* Shame on you, Jerome. Of course not. A good neighbor is dead. Let's try to show some emotion.

**LENORE.** You did it, didn't you Jerome? Admit it! You did it!

**JEROME.** Me? Where the hell is that coming from?

**LENORE.** You used that gun I found and you shot him.

**JEROME.** Are you insane? Why would I do that?

**LENORE.** Jealousy, rage, anger. The usual betrayed husband crap.

**FRANCINE.** Really? Wow, Jerome. You must really love me to commit murder. I'm really flattered.

**JEROME.** I didn't kill him. If anyone killed Anthony…

*(Pointing at* **LENORE***)*

…it was her. Their marriage was in the toilet. You told me that yourself. It was only a matter of time before he left her. And I wouldn't blame him one bit. She's actually nuttier than you. In fact, when she found that gun in Anthony's studio, I was sure he was planning to kill her with it because if I was him, I would.

**LENORE.** That's very harsh, Jerome. It'll take me more than a few days to get over that.

JEROME. *(To* LENORE*)* Too bad. Look, did you call the police?

LENORE. I don't know. Yes, no. I can't remember. I was hysterical and in a fog. I just remember running out of his studio screaming and coming over here.

JEROME. Okay, stay put. I'll call the police. And don't listen to her, Francine. I did not kill her husband and there's no way I can be blamed for it. No way.

FRANCINE. I hope so.

JEROME. Well, I know so. Try to stay calm. Both of you.

*(*JEROME *exits.)*

*(The two women watch him exit.* LENORE *takes a pair of gloves from her bathrobe pocket and slips them on.)*

LENORE. Not bad. A dead lover, a jealous husband and...

*(Pulls out the gun from her pocket)*

...the murder weapon with the jealous husband's finger prints on it.

*(She puts the gun in the desk drawer.)*

There. Right back where he put it.

*(Removing her gloves and going to* FRANCINE*)*

I think we just got rid of two jerks with one bullet. Now it's just you and me.

FRANCINE. Yes, just you and me.

*(They look at each other, then embrace and kiss.)*

*(Blackout)*


**End of Act I**

# ACT II

## Scene One

*(AT RISE: A spot light comes up on* **JEROME**, *now in an orange prison jumpsuit and handcuffs, sitting in a chair.)*

*(SOUND: Courtroom Buzz and then a gavel pounding three times calling for silence.)*

**JUDGE.** *(voice over)* Has the jury reached a verdict?

**JUROR.** *(voice over)* We have, your honor.

**JUDGE.** *(voice over)* Will the defendant please rise.

*(***JEROME*** stands.)*

*(voice over)* Will the jury foreman please read the verdict.

**JUROR.** *(voice over)* I will your honor. In the state's case against Jerome Teppel for the murder of Anthony Franklin, we the people, find the defendant guilty as charged.

*(SOUND: A few moments of Courtroom Buzz and then silence.)*

*(***JEROME*** is stunned, takes a beat and then screams at the top of his voice.)*

**JEROME.** I've been fuuuuucked!

*(Blackout)*

## Scene Two

*(TIME: Several months later. Early afternoon.)*

*(PLACE:* **SID DECKER**'s *Office.* **SID** *is behind his desk.* **LENORE** *and* **FRANCINE** *are seated in the chairs beside his desk. He leans back in his chair.)*

**SID**. So you two ladies seemed to have adjusted to single life quite well.

**LENORE**. Yes. We actually find everything in general to be much more pleasant without a man screwing it up.

**SID**. I've heard that from a number of women whose husbands are dead or rotting away in prison. Murder definitely does have its upside, doesn't it?

**FRANCINE**. For some, it certainly seems to be the case. I can't begin to tell you how delightfully surprised I was that my husband Jerome, living the frugal lifestyle that he seemed to enjoy, had amassed the hundreds of thousands of dollars that he had.

**SID**. Five hundred thousand to be exact. If we want to be exact.

**FRANCINE**. *(Surprised)* Yes. As a matter of fact, five hundred thousand if we want to be exact.

**SID**. As well as several more hundreds of thousands of dollars in stocks and bonds.

**FRANCINE**. Yes, as a second matter of fact, that too.

**SID**. Along with a substantial trust fund inheritance which places his net worth at, shall we say, a very cozy million and a half dollars and that, as his wife with Power of Attorney, you also now have access to.

**FRANCINE**. *(Further surprised by his knowledge)* Yes. It was another delightful surprise.

*(She shoots* **LENORE** *a worried look.)*

**SID**. Surprise? I think not, Mrs. Teppel. Especially since before you even met your husband, who is still not aware of this information, you worked as a file clerk in the law firm that represented his estate and had full access to all the information of his personal wealth. It turned out to be a wonderful place to find yourself a wealthy and eligible husband.

**FRANCINE.** Yes, but not against the law.

**SID.** No, you're right. Not against the law.

(*Turning to* **LENORE**)

And you, my dear recently widowed Mrs. Franklin. You seemed to have done equally as well, being the sole beneficiary of your late husband's million dollar double indemnity life insurance policy.

**LENORE.** You obviously have done your homework quite well, Sid. I never expected that of you.

**SID.** Of course you didn't. Otherwise you would have hired someone else. I was quite impressed by the fact that you were able to get an insurance company to insure that loser husband of yours for as much money as they did and not be a little bit suspicious.

**LENORE.** Well, working for an insurance company as I did these past few years, you do pick up on a few loopholes. I'm certain my late husband is resting much more peacefully knowing his beloved wife is well provided for.

**SID.** So, with both of you now being so financially well endowed it looks like the two of you are facing a pretty cushy life ahead of you.

**FRANCINE.** Yes, it certainly looks that way, Sidney.

**SID.** Well, let's hope nothing comes along to spoil it.

**LENORE.** Really? And what could possibly do that?

(**SID** *takes some eight-by-ten photos out of his desk drawer and shoves them in front of* **LENORE**.)

**SID.** Possibly these photos.

(**LENORE** *looks at them.*)

**LENORE.** Oh, my, my, my!

**SID.** I must say they came out pretty damn good. Your late husband dead on the floor with a bullet hole in his head, the gun in your hand.

**FRANCINE.** *(Looking at them)* Let me see. Oh, my, my, my, my, my, my. They really are quite impressive aren't they? It's no wonder these pictures came out so clearly. The smile on your face, Lenore, just lights up the room.

**LENORE.** Thank you.

**SID.** I'm glad you noticed that smile, Mrs. Teppel, because you had one very similar to it when the jury found your husband guilty of the murder. I have a photo of that too.

*(Pushes a photo in front of her)*

**FRANCINE.** Oh, my, my, my once again.

**LENORE.** Let me see yours.

*(Looks at photo)*

Very nice. You should have this made into Christmas cards and send one to Jerome.

**SID.** It would be very surprising to me if the D.A., presented with these photos, were to look over your testimony at your husband's trial and not see your involvement in this brilliant, but as you know, highly unlawful adventure.

**FRANCINE.** I would like to take this opportunity to say that you are making us very uncomfortable, Sid.

**LENORE.** You surprised me, Sid. I shot my husband that very night of the day we first saw you. I didn't expect you to be on the job that quickly.

**SID.** I know. Fortunately I've been around long enough to smell a set up. It was obvious that I was being hired only to serve as proof that Jerome was suspicious of his wife's infidelity, just in case testimony like that was needed. Setting up a camera in his studio only took a matter of minutes and fortunately I was able to do that while he was busy entertaining Mrs. Teppel in the back seat of his car.

(**LENORE** *gives* **FRANCINE** *a look.*)

**FRANCINE**. I swear Lenore. We were just listening to the radio.

(**SID** *pulls out a glass and bottle from his desk drawer and pours himself a drink.*)

**SID**. Mind if I have a drink?

**LENORE**. Please, drown yourself in it... Why now, Sid? Why not at the trial when an innocent man was being convicted?

**SID**. I needed to see what your game was. After some very extensive investigating, it seemed more than obvious it was never about anything else but the money.

**FRANCINE**. So, since you did not present this evidence at the trial, I assume your intentions towards us are not exactly the most honorable?

**SID**. No, I'm afraid they're not.

**LENORE**. Well, that's comforting to know. How much "not the most honorable" are we talking about?

**SID**. I believe with these pictures in my possession, half from each of you seems more than reasonable.

**FRANCINE**. You are an extremely unethical, immoral, despicable, low life slime ball, aren't you, Mr. Decker?

**SID**. Yes. But in this day and age, those things are looked at as highly desirable business attributes. Now, how shall we arrange payment?

(*A beat as he smiles at them.*)

(*The lights fade.*)

(*Blackout*)

## Scene Three

*(TIME: Several days later.)*

*(PLACE: A prison visitors room. The backdrop is a gray, cinder block wall.)*

*(**FRANCINE,** at Center Stage, holding a purse, sits patiently on a backless bench. After a few beats, **JEROME** enters. He is wearing the orange prison jump suit. His hands are handcuffed and his feet are shackled.)*

**JEROME.** *(Annoyed to see her)* Hello, Francine.

**FRANCINE.** Hello, Jerome. You're looking very...very rested.

**JEROME.** Yes, well, there's a good reason for that. I'm in solitary confinement. You're the first person I've seen in weeks. I'm surprised they even let me see you.

**FRANCINE.** Well, this is supposed to be a conjugal visit. They're very open-minded at the Department of Corrections so I told them that the two of us were trying to have a baby and that I was ovulating.

**JEROME.** You mean you've come here to have sex with me? Thank God. You have no idea how badly I need it. My nuts are the size of eggplants...and exactly the same color. By the way, how are you enjoying all my money?

**FRANCINE.** Very much, thank you. Never in my life did I ever think that one day I would own a BMW convertible and so much fine jewelry.

**JEROME.** Wonderful.

**FRANCINE.** Sit, Jerome. We need to talk a bit. So! I heard you tried to escape several times.

**JEROME.** Well, yeaaaah. That's why I'm in solitary confinement.

**FRANCINE.** I got the whole report. You tried to escape hiding in a laundry truck, you tried to escape hiding in a garbage truck, you tried tunneling under the wall, you tried crawling through the air condition system...

**JEROME.** The air conditioning attempt proved to be a big mistake. I caught pneumonia from that one. I was in the hospital for ten days.

**FRANCINE.** Still, Jerome, the fact that a not very creative person, such as yourself, came up with so many unusual attempts to escape, I must say I was very pleasantly surprised.

**JEROME.** Thanks but I really can't take all the credit. On movie night they've been showing us a lot of old gangster films so I get a lot of my ideas from those. Right now I'm trying to carve a machine gun out of soap. So far I have the trigger.

**FRANCINE.** Well, needless to say, I was very impressed with your determination. I hope your lack of success hasn't gotten you too discouraged.

**JEROME.** Never. I'm breaking out of here if it's the last thing I do. I was framed, Francine. Why the Judge and jury couldn't see that is beyond me.

**FRANCINE.** Be realistic, Jerome.

When the police got that mysterious phone call telling them to look in your desk and they found the murder weapon with your fingerprints on it and then with Anthony being my lover and you being so jealous, all the pieces just seemed to fall into place.

**JEROME.** I was screwed. And you didn't help things either. Taking the stand, crying hysterically and telling the jury how much you loved that moron, how could you do that?

**FRANCINE.** I was under oath, Jerome. I had to tell the truth.

**JEROME.** No you didn't. You're my wife. You didn't even have to testify. And then that jerk-off lawyer you hired to defend me. He was the worst lawyer you could have possibly gotten.

**FRANCINE.** He came highly recommended.

**JEROME.** He spoke no English.

**FRANCINE.** Yes, that proved to be a problem, didn't it?

JEROME. That was just one problem. He was also insane. The way he kept bending over and farting at the jury. It was disgusting.

FRANCINE. In all fairness, they were such a sour looking group, I think he was trying to disarm them with humor.

JEROME. And then when the nude painting of you was brought in as exhibit A, and while singing "O Sole Mio", he threw it on the courtroom floor and started dry-humping it, it was just too much.

FRANCINE. I know that made you a little uneasy but actually I was quite flattered. And you have to admit he had a beautiful voice.

JEROME. I couldn't help myself. I went for his throat.

FRANCINE. Oh, that was so exciting. It took seven guards to get you off of him. You were on national television that whole night.

JEROME. After that, I didn't have a chance.

FRANCINE. I know. On the plus side, the whole trial only took forty minutes so it's not like you had to live with that much anxiety. By the way, would you believe that nude painting of me sold on ebay for sixteen thousand dollars.

JEROME. You're kidding? To who?

FRANCINE. Some minister down south. I got another artist to paint a halo over my head and add a huge cross in the background. In next year's church calendar, I'm going to be Miss February.

JEROME. *(Sighs in disgust)* Why are you here, Francine?

FRANCINE. Because I have good news for you, Jerome. I'm over him.

JEROME. Who?

FRANCINE. Anthony. The guy you killed and who I once loved with all my heart.

JEROME. I didn't kill him.

**FRANCINE**. Regardless. What happened between me and Anthony simply turned out to be one of those foolish, silly, immature crushes. You know how those stories go. I was impressed by his talent, he was fantastic in the sack, et cetera, et cetera. But these past few months without him or you around I've had time to think things through and guess what, Jerome. Anthony's out, you're in.

**JEROME**. Anthony's out? Anthony's dead! And the only place I'm in is an eight by ten prison cell. Jesus, Francine, you are wackier than I even thought you were. I got thirty years to life for god's sake, plus they keep adding on five years every time I try to break out of this hell hole. By the time I do get released you'll be a hundred and eighty years old. Why the hell would I want a woman that age?

**FRANCINE**. Stop it, Jerome. You're going to be out of here sooner than you think.

**JEROME**. And how is that going to be arranged?

**FRANCINE**. Very simply. The next time you attempt a break out you'll have this.

*(She opens her purse and takes out a handgun and hands it to him.)*

**JEROME**. A gun! A real gun!

**FRANCINE**. Yes. I got it at Larry's gun shop. I had to pay full price but I felt you were worth it.

**JEROME**. A gun! Oh, wow. How did you sneak a gun in here?

**FRANCINE**. I was very lucky. They didn't give me an anal cavity search.

**JEROME**. Yuk!

*(He quickly holds the gun with two fingers.)*

**FRANCINE**. No, it's okay. It was in a plastic bag and I removed it in the ladies room.

JEROME. Wow, Francine. Hiding a gun up your butt. Maybe you do love me after all. What about bullets?

FRANCINE. They're already in the gun.

JEROME. They are? My god, you could have blown a hole in your ass, although that would be redundant, wouldn't it?

FRANCINE. *(Rises)* Call me as soon as you get out, Jerome. We'll have dinner.

JEROME. Yeah, yeah. I will. It probably won't be for a couple of days. I want to wait until my laundry comes back. I've been walking around without underwear and it's very uncomfortable.

FRANCINE. Whenever. Good luck, Jerome.

*(She kisses him on the cheek and exits.)*

JEROME. Yeah, so long, Francine. Thanks for the G-U-N.

*(He starts out. Then stops.)*

Jesus, we forgot to have sex. She's going to be so disappointed when she gets home.

*(He shoves the gun in his pocket and hobbles off.)*

*(Blackout)*

## Scene Four

*(The stage is dark.)*

*(Prison sirens go off signaling a breakout. Search lights scan the stage. Machine gunfire, rifle shots and barking dogs are heard. A desperate* **JEROME**, *with a gun in his hand, is suddenly caught in one of the search lights. He has a terrified look on his face. More gunfire. He darts out of the light. More gunfire, barking dogs and more search lights. The volume lowers and then silence.)*

*(Blackout)*

## Scene Five

*(TIME: The next evening.)*

*(PLACE: The* **TEPPEL** *living room.)*

*(Lights up on* **FRANCINE** *and* **LENORE** *seated Down Stage Center. They are in bathrobes. Underneath,* **FRANCINE** *has on her costume for the next scene. They both wear a raised shiny gold halo on their head. Smiling angelically at the audience, they rise and holding hands, approach the front of the stage and begin singing "Amazing Grace" by John Newton, 1779.)*

**FRANCINE.**

AMAZING GRACE! HOW SWEET THE SOUND.

**LENORE.**

THAT SAVED A WRETCH LIKE ME.

**FRANCINE.**

I ONCE WAS LOST,

**LENORE.**

BUT NOW I'M FOUND.

**BOTH.**

WAS BLIND BUT NOW WE SEE.

*(At that moment* **FRANCINE**'s *cell phone rings. The women stop singing and* **FRANCINE** *takes the phone out of her pocket.)*

**FRANCINE.** Hello. Jerome! I knew it was you. I saw on this evening's news you escaped. Good boy! I knew you could do it.

*(***FRANCINE** *gives* **LENORE** *a thumbs up sign.)*

Listen, I have great news for you. Remember Sid Decker? Yes, the detective you and Lenore saw. Well, he says he has new evidence that can prove your innocence. Isn't that wonderful? As soon as I heard you escaped I called him. He wants to see us at his office tomorrow morning at ten. No, don't come here. It's not a good idea. Why not? Well, I just had the carpets cleaned and they're still wet.

*(LENORE give FRANCINE an approval nod.)*

Look, why, don't you find an all night movie theatre and spend the night there. Of course you'll be safe. Just don't sit next to anyone in a raincoat. I'll see you tomorrow. Yes, Jerome. Yes, I love you too.

*(She hangs up and shakes her head sadly.)*

God, men are so naive. Every now and then I almost feel sorry for them.

LENORE. That's one of your problems. You have too big a heart.

FRANCINE. I know. It's one of my major flaws.

*(They both sigh, hold hands and once more like little angels, return to the song.)*

BOTH.
'TIS GRACE HAS BROUGHT US SAFE THUS FAR,
AND GRACE WILL LEAD US HOME.

*(Their angelic smiles widen.)*

*(Blackout)*

## Scene Six

*(TIME: The next morning.)*

*(PLACE:* **SID DECKER**'s *office.)*

*(***SID***, in his swivel chair, is turned facing the window behind his desk, apparently staring out of it.* **FRANCINE** *sits patiently in a chair. She is wearing gloves and has a purse.* **JEROME** *enters. He is still in his orange prison jump suit.* **FRANCINE** *rushes to him and hugs him.)*

FRANCINE. Darling.

JEROME. Sweetheart. I would have been here sooner but I got stopped by a cop for throwing a gum wrapper on the street.

FRANCINE. Yes, our mayor's very serious about keeping the city clean. He's definitely getting my vote again.

*(***JEROME*** *spots* **SID***. He goes to him.)*

JEROME. This is the guy I want to see. All right, Decker. You said you can prove I'm innocent, let's hear what you've got.

*(***JEROME*** *swings* **SID***'s chair around revealing a bullet hole with blood on* **SID***'s forehead.)*

Holy Crap! There's a bullet hole in his head.

*(***SID*** *slumps forward, his head falling to the desk.)*

He's dead.

FRANCINE. Yes, I know. Isn't that just awful? But don't worry. I called the police. They should be here any minute.

JEROME. Oh, good. No, wait! Not good. That's the worst thing you could have done. They're going to find me here and send me back to prison.

FRANCINE. Oh, my. You're right. Why didn't I think of that?

*(SOUND: Police sirens. Cars pulling up to the bldg.)*

*(***JEROME*** *looks out the window.)*

JEROME. Oh, jeez! There must be two dozen cop cars that just pulled up. What should I do, Francine?

FRANCINE. Do you still have the gun you escaped with?

JEROME. No. I sold it to a high school kid to get money for the movie.

FRANCINE. That's okay. I have another.

(FRANCINE *opens her purse, takes out a gun and puts it in his hand.*)

Here! I believe in you Jerome. Take this one and make a break for it.

JEROME. Are you crazy. With all those cops down there I haven't got a chance in hell of getting out of here alive.

FRANCINE. I know, but I still like the odds.

JEROME. Hey. This gun is warm. As if it's just been fired.

FRANCINE. It has.

JEROME. It has?

FRANCINE. *(Indicating* SID*)* Yes. I just shot Sid with it.

JEROME. You did?

(JEROME *looks at the gun, looks at* FRANCINE, *looks at the gun again, looks at* FRANCINE *again.* FRANCINE *smiles and nods.*)

FRANCINE. I did.

JEROME. *(Horrified)* With *this* gun?

FRANCINE. With that gun which unfortunately now has your fingerprints on it.

COP. *(voice over) (On megaphone)* All right, Teppel. Come out with your hands up or you're a dead man.

(JEROME *looks at gun, then at* FRANCINE, *then back at gun and then to audience.*)

JEROME. *(Screaming)* Once more I've been fuuuuucked!

*(Blackout)*

## Scene Seven

*(A spotlight is on **LENORE** at Downstage Center. She addresses the audience.)*

**LENORE**. Fairness! I need to speak about fairness. As far as I'm concerned, that word has no business even being in the dictionary because what's fair to one person can never, ever be fair to another person and the minute you hear anyone say "Well, that sounds fair", you can bet your golden ass it isn't – even if it's you saying it. Someone, some how is getting screwed in the deal no matter how insignificant.

Two bags of M&M's. The same size, the same price. I can guarantee you, one bag will have more green "M"s than the other. Petty, yes. Fair? Not in my book.

Two watches. One costing six dollars. The other, sixty thousand dollars. Yet, they keep the same exact time. Fair? Once more, I think not. Out of common decency shouldn't the cheap one be a little less accurate?

A marathon race. Twenty six miles for everyone. Fair? Not for the people with the shorter legs.

Is it fair that for the same amount of money...

*(Points to someone in back row)*

...you paid for your seat tonight,

*(Points to someone in front row)*

...this person has a much better seat?

You see what I'm getting at? There is always someone getting the edge.

And this is what pisses me off the most. Why is it men's private parts have such nicer names than women's private parts? Mr. Happy. Mr. Twinkie. Smiling Dick and the Twins. God, they sound like Saturday morning cartoon shows. Yet we women get stuck with some of the most disgusting and degrading nomenclatures. Tuna Taco. Bearded Oyster. Salmon Canyon. Give me a break. Not only is it disgusting, but it's very confusing.

Does that give fish a good name or a bad name? God, why am I cursed with such depth?

Fairness! A myth. A fantasy. A delusion. And here is the sad reality. If we can't find it in these insignificant little areas I just brought up, how can we expect to find it on greater levels like in our government, our justice system... Fox News? The answer is, we can't and we won't and we shouldn't expect to. Unfairness is part of our nature, our DNA, our inherent life form.

So please, do yourself a favor. Don't hold your breath looking for fairness tonight. It ain't gonna happen. Thank you. We will now continue with the play.

*(Blackout)*

## Scene Eight

*(TIME: Months later. Afternoon)*

*(PLACE: Death Row visitors room.)*

*(**FRANCINE** is waiting in a chair. **JEROME** enters. His hands are shackled and he has a ball and chain around one leg that he drags with him. He wears a black and white stripped prison uniform with a matching cap.)*

**FRANCINE.** Hello, Jerome. Long time no see.

**JEROME.** Yes. Eight months. And I've enjoyed every minute of it. Why are you here?

**FRANCINE.** To apologize, Jerome. To tell you how sorry I am that I put you through what I put you through. I was wrong. Very, very wrong and I'm sorry. Very, very sorry.

**JEROME.** You're sorry? You're sorry? Damn it, Francine. Thanks to you, in two weeks I'm going to the electric chair.

**FRANCINE.** I know. Tough break. I was surprised you used the same lawyer.

**JEROME.** He was the only one that would defend me. But I had time to think this whole thing through. It was you and her together, wasn't it? The two of you were both in this frame up from the start.

**FRANCINE.** Well, yeaaaah. I'm surprised it took you so long to figure it out.

**JEROME.** And now a sweet, kind, loving, stupid, innocent CPA is going to meet his maker. And when I do I'm kicking him right in the balls.

**FRANCINE.** Come, on Jerome. Try to put a more positive spin on things. Life is never as bad as it seems.

**JEROME.** Are you crazy? They're going to fry me like a chicken. Ahh, the hell with it. I can't handle it anymore. I never thought I'd say this but I'm actually looking forward to death.

FRANCINE. That's always been your problem, Jerome. Every time you're faced with issues of any kind, instead of dealing with them, you turn your back and run.

JEROME. Issues! I never had any issues until you came into my life.

FRANCINE. Yes, and if anything, you should thank me for that. Don't you see, Jerome, it's issues that keep our blood flowing, it's issues that provide the adrenaline our body and mind need to make every day different and stimulating and exciting. It's issues that keep us charged up and alive. Look at you! You're experiencing a whole new adventure. You're no longer in that day in and day out CPA rut. You've finally unshackled your soul and broken free.

JEROME. *(Picks up his iron ball)* Do me a favor, Francine. Bring your head a little closer to me. I want to bash it with this iron ball. I promise I'll be very careful not to mess your hair.

FRANCINE. Please, Jerome. Try to get off the pity pot and stop that annoying whining of yours. I'm about to tell you something very important. Something that will change your whole life. This thing between me and Lenore, it isn't working out.

JEROME. Good.

FRANCINE. I'm very, very unhappy.

JEROME. Double good.

FRANCINE. No matter what I do, no matter how hard I try, I can't find that magic place in me called contentment. Sometimes I ask myself, is it "you"?

JEROME. How can it be me? I've been in prison for eight months.

FRANCINE. No, no, Jerome. I'm asking me, not you. I'm using "you" as a metaphor for "me". Try to pay attention. Okay, so here I am. I tried having a relationship with a man, that didn't work.

JEROME. You mean me?

**FRANCINE.** No, I mean Anthony. Will you please try to stop thinking about yourself for at least a few minutes.

**JEROME.** Sorry.

**FRANCINE.** I tried having a relationship with a woman, Lenore, that didn't work. Neither seemed to be the answer.

**JEROME.** So?

**FRANCINE.** So I've come to the conclusion that maybe I need to split the difference and that leaves you again, Jerome.

**JEROME.** Francine, what if you lie down on the floor and let me step on your face. You have no idea what pleasure that will bring me.

**FRANCINE.** Shut up, Jerome and listen. I've made up my mind to leave her. I'm going to Brazil and I'm planning to take three things with me. Your money, her money, and you. Just think, Jerome. We'll have over three million dollars. We'll never have to worry about anything for the rest of our lives.

**JEROME.** You're taking Lenore's money too? You really are a scheming bitch aren't you, Francine?

**FRANCINE.** Damn it, Jerome, can you ever focus on the positive? I'm trying to reach out to you. Brazil, Jerome! Land of eternal romance, a country exploding in devil-may-care lust and passion... Sin, sex and samba. You and me on the beach, every day, every night, making love.

**JEROME.** Love! I haven't really had any since they executed my cell mate, Bubba Finch. For a serial killer he was a fairly nice guy. Great legs.

**FRANCINE.** Say yes, Jerome. I beg you, say yes.

**JEROME.** Francine, I wouldn't trust you if my life depended on it.

**FRANCINE.** Well, right now it actually does. So are you in or out?

**JEROME.** Get real will you. This is a higher security prison than the last one I was in. No one has ever broken out of here. There are four, twelve inch thick cement walls between me and freedom.

**FRANCINE.** No problem, Jerome. I have that all worked out. You'll be out of here in no time at all. Here. Take these.

*(She stands with her back to the audience and lifts the front of her skirt, leans over and with great effort, pulls four grenades from under her skirt, placing them in JEROME's cupped hands as he looks on in amazement.)*

One, two, three, four. One for each wall.

*(She lowers her skirt and turns to him.)*

**JEROME.** Hand grenades? You hid four hand grenades in your…your wapa-palooza? How the hell did you do that?

**FRANCINE.** It wasn't easy. I practiced for six weeks. I started with plums and worked my way up to grapefruits.

**JEROME.** Wow, you're very lucky. The next size fruit was cantaloupe. Congratulations. You should have no trouble having babies.

**FRANCINE.** Oh, Jerome, I promise you this time we are going to have such a wonderful life together.

**JEROME.** I find that very hard to believe.

*(**FRANCINE** takes the grenades from **JEROME** and places them in his pants pockets.)*

**FRANCINE.** Well, don't. This is the first time anything in my life made real sense. We are two needy people. I need you and you need me. You can't find a better reason for a healthy relationship than that. Now, I have it all worked out for you.

*(She takes some bills and a drivers license from her purse and stuffs them in his pants pocket.)*

Here's your driver's license and several hundred dollars. Once you blast your way out of here you'll rent a car and pick me up. I'll be all packed and ready to go.

JEROME. We're going to drive to Brazil?

FRANCINE. We have to. You're a fugitive. They'll be checking bus stations and airports everywhere for you. Driving makes the most sense.

JEROME. I don't know. I'm worried about that lunatic Lenore. She's not going to like this.

FRANCINE. Not to worry. Leave Lenore to me.

JEROME. You're not going to...

FRANCINE. Kill her? Of course not. What kind of person do you think I am? But I promise she won't be a problem.

JEROME. This is all coming at me much too fast.

FRANCINE. It's a no brainer, Jerome. You have nothing to lose. The state is about to turn you into a pot roast. Good luck. I'll be waiting for you with a bag of money and a life that most people can only dream about. It'll be wonderful.

*(She kisses him passionately on the lips.)*

How was that?

JEROME. Almost as good as Bubba.

FRANCINE. Goodbye, my sweet darling.

*(She starts to limp off.)*

JEROME. You're limping.

FRANCINE. You try shoving four hand grenades up your vagina, Jerome and let's see how well you walk.

*(She exits.)*

JEROME. *(Confused)* A vagina? A vagina? What the hell is a vagina?

*(With the grenades bulging out of his pocket, **JEROME** lifts his ball and hobbles off.)*

*(Blackout)*

## Scene Nine

*(The second escape)*

*(The stage is dark.)*

*(Suddenly there is an explosion. Sirens go off. Search lights scan the stage. Machine gunfire, rifle shots, and barking dogs are heard. A second explosion and we see a desperate* **JEROME** *with two grenades in his hand caught in one of the search lights. More gunfire. He dodges out of the light. More gunfire and barking dogs and then a third explosion and then more gunfire.* **JEROME,** *with a terrified look and now with his last grenade, is again caught in a spot. He pauses for a beat and addresses the audience.)*

**JEROME.** It's tough, but still not as tough as marriage.

*(He darts out of the light. More gunfire, barking dogs and then a fourth explosion and then silence.)*

*(Blackout)*

## Scene Ten

*(TIME: Later that night.)*

*(PLACE: The* **TEPPEL** *living room.)*

*(Lights up on the desk. A cell phone on the desk starts to ring.* **FRANCINE** *carrying a small satchel enters from bedroom. She places the satchel on the desk and answers the cell phone.)*

**FRANCINE.** Jerome. I knew it was you. Where are you? Good. Park the car in front of the house and come in. The door's unlocked. There are a few things I need you to help carry to the car. Yes, I took care of Lenore. I put half a dozen sleeping pills in her soup at dinner. What kind of soup? Tomato soup, what does it matter? No, there's none left over. No, she didn't suspect anything. Yes, I have all the money. Yes, I love you too. No, we'll have sex when we get to Brazil. Yes, I promise.

*(Hangs up)*

What a shmuck.

*(She then dials 911 and speaks in panic)*

9-1-1? Quick! 1542 Oakdale Avenue. My husband, Jerome Teppel, has broken out of jail and just shot my lesbian lover dead. Hurry. What? Twenty minutes. You can't get here sooner? Yes, I know about the budget cuts. Okay, okay, do your best.

*(She hangs up. Disdainfully.)*

Damn! What if there was a real emergency? Oh, well, now for Jerome's third victim.

*(She takes a gun out of the desk drawer and sighs.)*

Poor Jerome. He was just out of his league.

*(Walks towards bedroom with gun)*

I hate to do this to you, Lenore, but if I don't I know you'll track me down to the ends of the earth!

*(She exits.)*

*(After a few moments of silence there is a gun shot. A few beats later **LENORE** enters from the bedroom. She is wearing a bathrobe and has a gun in her hand.)*

**LENORE.** Why are relationships so damn difficult?

*(She puts the gun down on the desk. The front door opens and **JEROME** enters. He looks at **LENORE**.)*

**JEROME.** Done?

**LENORE.** Done.

*(**JEROME** goes to the satchel on the desk and opens it.)*

**JEROME.** Lots of money in there.

**LENORE.** Everything we both owned. Poor Francine. She really thought she was going to get away with it.

**JEROME.** Yeah. Well, she'll just have to learn to deal with disappointment won't she.

*(Pulls out an airline ticket from the satchel and looks through it)*

Look at this. One, one-way airline ticket to Brazil leaving tonight. What a double crosser. I knew she couldn't be trusted.

**LENORE.** Of course she couldn't. She was a hard core sociopath. My mother was one. They say it's genetic but luckily it skipped me.

**JEROME.** What I don't understand is, if she was going to knock you off and pin it on me, why would she need to get out of the country?

**LENORE.** It makes perfect sense, Jerome.

She would have been connected to three murders. How dumb can the cops continue to be before they start asking questions? That's one of the reasons why I decided to go with you.

*(**LENORE** approaches **JEROME** from behind and laying her head on his shoulder, she puts her arms around him.)*

The other reason was, I always had a crush on you.

JEROME. Really?

LENORE. Yes. And then when you warned me about Francine's intentions I knew you felt something for me too.

JEROME. To be perfectly honest, Lenore, I'm not sure I do.

LENORE. Sure you do, Jerome. I picked up on that immediately, no matter how much you went out of your way to pretend you didn't. Now, it's not that I didn't enjoy my intimacy with your wife. I think we both did for the most part. I believe the difficulty stemmed from the fact that we both got our periods at the same time. For five days a month you needed a buzz saw to cut the tension in this house.

JEROME. Glad I missed that.

LENORE. But now it's just you and me and all the money we'll ever need. Oh, Jerome, we are going to be magic together.

JEROME. You think so? Well, maybe it can work out. I have been pretty lonely and you know what they say? Any port in a storm.

LENORE. My feelings exactly. Well, I'll go change into some clothes and we'll be off.

*(She hands him the gun.)*

Here, take this gun. We'll toss it in the first river we come to.

**(JEROME** *looks at the gun in his hand. There is a moment of déjà vu. Is he about to get screwed again?)*

By the way, did you pick up the sandwiches like I asked you?

JEROME. Yeah. They're in the car. I got a ham on rye for me and a Swiss cheese for you.

LENORE. Damn it, Jerome. I didn't say Swiss cheese. I said grilled cheese.

JEROME. Are you sure? I swear you said Swiss cheese.

LENORE. I hate Swiss cheese. It tastes like wax. How the hell can you get Swiss cheese and grilled cheese mixed up?

JEROME. All right, all right. I'll eat your Swiss cheese. You can have my ham on rye.

LENORE. Does it have mayo on it?

JEROME. Yes, it has mayo on it. I like mayo.

LENORE. For God's sake, Jerome. How many times do you have to be reminded that I can only eat mayo *in* something and not *on* something. Can't you keep anything straight in that brain of yours? I'll be ready to leave in five minutes.

*(She exits to bedroom.* JEROME *looks at the gun again, then pauses for a moment to think.)*

JEROME. You know, Lenore. I don't really know whether or not, somewhere down the road, you're planning to screw me over like you women have constantly been doing. But I can see, no matter what, it's not going to work out between us because your friggen eating habits would drive me crazy.

LENORE. *(Offstage)* What? I can't hear you. Speak louder, Jerome? What were you saying?

JEROME. *(Louder)* Just this Lenore.

I think in the long run this is going to provide a much more happy and satisfying ending for everyone.

*(Lifting his gun,* JEROME *exits to the bedroom.)*

*(SOUND: Gunshot)*

*(There is a beat and* JEROME *re-enters holding the gun. He blows at the barrel to cool it off and addresses the audience.)*

Boy, if I didn't spend time in the pen learning to become a hardened criminal, I never could have handled this.

*(He sticks the gun in his pocket, picks up the bag of money and addresses the audience.)*

One bag of money, one rented getaway car outside with brand new license plates that I made in prison myself and which I'm very proud of. Plus now I get to eat both sandwiches. Anyway, I'll be heading to a place that's too dangerous for anyone to ever come looking for me. Either Mexico, Columbia, El Salvador or better yet, New Jersey. I'm not telling you exactly where because as you've seen, in this world you can't trust anyone.

Then while I'm there, I'm going to write a book about all this with a much more exciting ending. I'm going to throw in a car chase, gun fighting, a wonderful sex scene in a cheesy motel, and then sell it to the movies and make even more money. Then I will change my name and open accounting offices all over the world because once a CPA, always a CPA. Well, I'm off. Do me a favor. When the cops come, stall them as long as you can. Nice meeting you.

*(With the satchel of money, **JEROME** exits. The stage darkens. There is a beat. We hear a car start and then with a roaring engine and squealing tires, peel off.)*

*(MUSIC: Stirring, triumphant, upbeat, victorious music sneaks in, growing louder and louder. Several beats later and also sneaking in and growing louder are police sirens approaching, yet the overwhelming victorious music leaves us with the feeling that **JEROME** has safely escaped.)*

*(Blackout)*


**The End**

# PROPS

## ACT I

### Scene 1 – The Teppel Living Room

Calculator with paper roll
Stack of bills, receipts
Pencil
Pad of paper

### Scene 2 – Park Bench

A bag containing:
  2 cups of coffee
  Turkey sandwich
  Roast beef sandwich
  Paper napkins

### Scene 3 – The Teppel Living Room – Another Area

Smith Wesson 38 revolver
Magazine

### Scene 4 – Detective's Office

Bottle of whiskey
Whiskey glass
Paper bag containing:
  2 cups of coffee
  Tuna salad sandwich
  Chicken salad on pumpernickel
  Prune Danish

### Scene 5 – The Teppel Living Room

Smith Wesson 38 revolver

## ACT II

### Scene 1 – Courtroom

Handcuffs

### Scene 2 – Detective's Office

Bottle of whiskey
Whiskey glass (From Act I, Scene 4)
Several 8x10 photos described in scene.

# PROPS – CONTINUED

### Scene 3 – Prison Visitors Room

Handcuffs
Feet shackles
Purse
Smith Wesson 38 revolver

### Scene 4 – 1st Prison Break

Smith Wesson 38 revolver

### Scene 5 – The Teppel Living Room

FRANCINE's cell phone

### Scene 6 – Detective's Office

Smith Wesson 38 revolver

### Scene 7 – Lenore's Monologue

None

### Scene 8 – Death Row Visitors Room

Hand shackles
Leg ball and chain
4 hand grenades
Purse
Several monetary bills and drivers license (in purse)

### Scene 9 – 2nd Prison Break

2 hand grenades

### Scene 10 – The Teppel Living Room

Small satchel with stash of money and plane ticket
FRANCINE's cell phone
Smith Wesson 38 revolver

# COSTUMES

## ACT I

### Scene 1 – The Teppel Living Room
**JEROME** – Pants, white dress shirt, sleeves rolled up, tie
**FRANCINE** – Bathrobe, slippers

### Scene 2 – Park Bench
**LENORE** – Business dress
**JEROME** – Suit, white shirt, tie

### Scene 3 – The Teppel Living Room – Another Area
**FRANCINE** – Skirt, blouse, shoes
**JEROME** – Pants, shirt, button down sweater

### Scene 4 – Detective's Office
**SID** – Seedy looking suit, wrinkled shirt, loose tie
**LENORE** – A different business dress
**JEROME** – Suit and Tie

### Scene 5 – The Teppel Living Room
**JEROME** – Bathrobe, slippers
**FRANCINE** – Bathrobe, slippers
**LENORE** – Bathrobe, slippers, gloves in pocket

## ACT II

### Scene 1 – Courtroom
**JEROME** – Orange prison jumpsuit

### Scene 2 – Detective's Office
**SID** – Same seedy suit as in Act I, different loose fitting tie
**FRANCINE** – Elegant daytime dress, shoes, purse
**LENORE** – Elegant daytime dress, shoes, purse

### Scene 3 – Prison Visitors Room
**FRANCINE** – Conservative dress, shoes, purse
**JEROME** – Orange prison jumpsuit

### Scene 4 – 1st Prison Break
**JEROME** – Orange prison jumpsuit

# COSTUMES – CONTINUED

### Scene 5 – The Teppel Living Room

**FRANCINE** and **LENORE** – Matching bathrobes, 2 shiny halos to wear on their heads

### Scene 6 – Detective's Office

**SID** – Same seedy suit as in Act I, different loose fitting tie
**FRANCINE** – Elegant daytime dress, shoes, purse
**JEROME** – Orange prison jumpsuit

### Scene 7 – Lenore's Monologue

**LENORE** – Casually and comfortably dressed

### Scene 8 – Death Row Visitor Room

**FRANCINE** – Fluffy long skirt and blouse
**JEROME** – Stripped prison clothes with a matching cap

### Scene 9 – 2nd Prison Break

**JEROME** – Same as in Scene 8

### Scene 10 – The Teppel Living Room

**FRANCINE** – Pants Suit
**JEROME** – Same as in Scene 8
**LENORE** – Bathrobe, slippers

Lightning Source UK Ltd.
Milton Keynes UK
UKOW05f0918080317
296132UK00001B/11/P